FLORENCE AND ERIC
TAKE THE CAKE

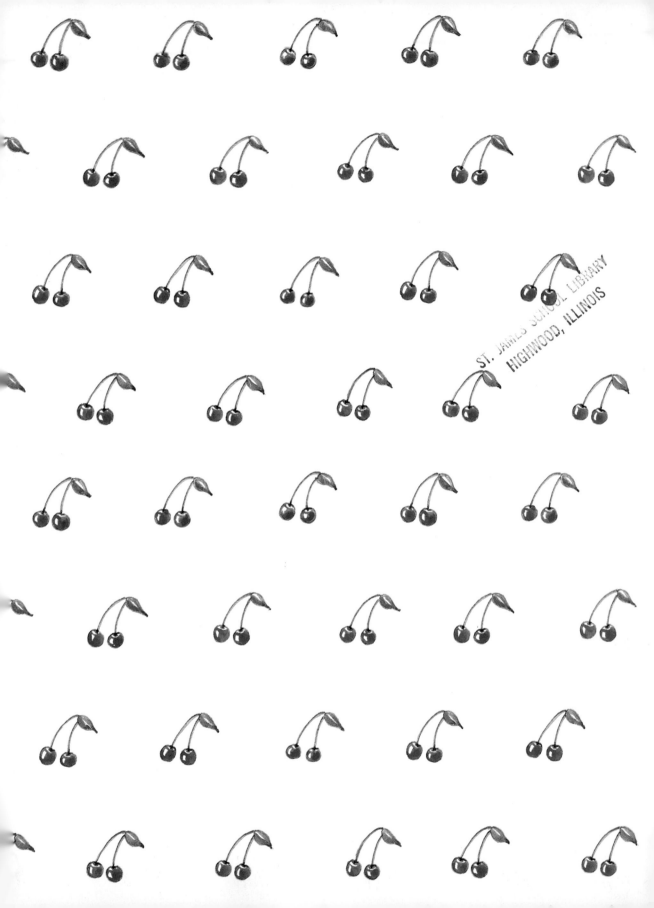

FLORENCE AND ERIC TAKE THE CAKE

Jocelyn Wild

Dial Books for Young Readers *New York*

First published in the United States by
Dial Books for Young Readers
A Division of Penguin Books USA Inc.
375 Hudson Street
New York, New York 10014

Published in Great Britain by William Heinemann Ltd.
Copyright © 1987 by Jocelyn Wild
All rights reserved
Library of Congress Catalog Card Number: 87-639
Printed in Hong Kong
First Pied Piper Printing 1990
N
1 3 5 7 9 10 8 6 4 2

A Pied Piper Book is a registered trademark of
Dial Books for Young Readers,
a division of Penguin Books USA Inc.,
® TM 1,163,686 and ® TM 1,054,312.

FLORENCE AND ERIC TAKE THE CAKE
is published in a hardcover edition by
Dial Books for Young Readers.
ISBN 0-8037-0676-6

*For Granny
and Grandpa Wild*

This is Rosemary Cottage where Granny and Grandpa Mutton live. It's summer vacation and Florence and her little brother Eric have come for a visit.

This morning Granny is very busy. The ladies from the Little Nibbling Knitting Circle are meeting here and Granny must tidy up.

Florence and Eric want to help Granny get ready.
Mother has told them to make sure they
do everything they can for Granny and Grandpa.

Just then the telephone rings. It is Miss Lavinia
Bleating. She's made her heavenly angel food cake
for the Knitting Circle this afternoon. But now
she has come down with the most frightful cold
and can't come.

"Oh, take care, my dear," says Granny. "What if I send Florence and Eric for the cake? It's about time they had some fresh air."

"Good idea. I'll leave it in the hall," Miss Bleating replies. "Tell Florence to walk straight in. The door will be open."

Miss Lavinia has spent all morning icing the cake with her favorite marshmallow frosting. At last it's finished!

She leaves the cake in the hall and goes upstairs
to lie down. Poor Miss Lavinia doesn't feel well at all.

A moment later Lavinia's sister Muriel comes home. She has been out shopping for a new hat to wear to *The Baa Baa of Seville*, her favorite opera. Muriel is going to town to see it this evening.

Muriel loves the opera and has a very fine voice herself. She keeps it in perfect pitch by practicing in the bathtub every day. So when the front door opens, she doesn't hear it.

Florence and Eric have come for the cake. Eric sees the box on the hall table, lifts it down, and takes it to Florence.

Florence checks to make sure the cake's inside
and puts it in her basket.
She carries it herself – Eric might drop it.

19

Promptly at four-thirty the taxi arrives to take Muriel to the train station.

In two shakes

she is dressed

and ready
to go.

There is just her hat to put on.

And what an elegant hat it is. Why! Those cherries look almost real! She puts it firmly on her head.

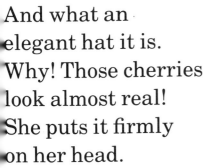

AAAARGH!

Oh, no! What a mess! This isn't her hat at all! It's a *cake!* A horrid sloppy sticky cake! Muriel lets out a very loud scream.

23

Meanwhile the ladies of the Knitting Circle have been very busy all afternoon knitting sweaters for poor orphan lambs and now it is time for some refreshments.

Everyone is looking forward to a nice cup of tea
and a slice of dear Lavinia's cake. It looks almost
too good to eat.

But, oh dear, how tough the cake is! How dry!
Mrs. Woolly-Jumper has just broken a tooth on
one of the cherries. And Mrs. Scrag is choking.

There's no doubt about it. The cake is uneatable.

But Florence thinks it makes a lovely hat.
And Eric agrees.

Jocelyn Wild

has collaborated with her husband, Robin, on several titles, including *The Bears' ABC Book* and *The Bears' Counting Book*, but *Florence and Eric Take the Cake*, a *Reading Rainbow* Feature Selection, is her first solo turn. Ms. Wild was born in India and studied languages at London University. She and her husband have two children, Ben and Tom. The Wilds live in the English countryside.